# Ranger

Saddle Up Series
Book 48

Dave and Pat Sargent are longtime residents of Prairie Grove, Arkansas. Dave, a fourth-generation dairy farmer, began writing in early December 1990. Pat, a former teacher, began writing in the fourth grade. They enjoy the outdoors and have a real love for animals.

# Ranger

Saddle Up Series
Book 48

## By Dave and Pat Sargent

## Beyond "The End"
By Sue Rogers

Illustrated by Jane Lenoir

Ozark Publishing, Inc.
P.O. Box 228
Prairie Grove, AR 72753

Cataloging-in-Publication Data

Sargent, Dave, 1941–
    Ranger / by Dave and Pat Sargent ;
illustrated by Jane Lenoir.—Prairie Grove, AR :
Ozark Publishing, c2004.
        p.  cm.  (Saddle up series ; 48)

    "Be honest"—Cover.
    SUMMARY:  Ranger, Allan Pinkerton's
horse, is saved from a horse thief by his master.
Contains factual information about olive grullo
horses.
        ISBN 1-56763-709-4 (hc)
                1-56763-710-8 (pbk)


    1. Horses—Juvenile Fiction.  [1. Horses—
Juvenile fiction.  2. Horses—Fiction.  3. Pinkerton,
Allan, 1819–1884—Fiction.]  I. Sargent, Pat, 1936–
II. Lenoir, Jane, 1950– ill.  III. Title.  IV. Series.

    PZ10.3.S243Ran 2004
    [Fic]--dc21                          2001005625

Printed in the United States of America

# Inspired by

beautiful blue slate-colored horses with dark heads we see as we travel.

# Dedicated to

all children
who love unripe olives!

# Foreword

Ranger the olive grullo's boss is Allan Pinkerton, who owns the best detective agency in the world. The olive grullo is horrified when he learns of a secret plot to assassinate president-elect Abraham Lincoln.

# Contents

If you would like to have the authors of the Saddle Up Series visit your school, free of charge, call 1-800-321-5671 or 1-800-960-3876.

# One

# The Olive Grullo

A bolt of lightning streaked across the sky above the Rocking S Horse Ranch. A puff of smoke and dust billowed into the air as it hit a large tree on the hill above the barn. And a split second later, deafening thunder boomed across the land. Ranger the olive grullo knew that this was going to be a bad storm.

"Everybody okay?" he neighed loudly.

"I-I think so," the palomino replied.

"Good," Ranger said in a loud voice. "Let's take cover under the shed on the south side of the barn."

Raindrops were pelting the ground as the herd of horses loped toward the shed. But they were unable to reach safety before large hailstones began crashing down upon them.

"Don't stop!" Ranger yelled. "We will be okay when we get to the shed. Run!"

Moments later the last horse was beneath the roof of the shed.

The roar from the pounding hail was too loud for the horses to hear each other, so they did not try to talk. They stood quietly with their ears turned away from the roof. They would have to wait for the storm to subside. They stood in silence for three or four minutes before the large white pebbles of ice were replaced with heavy rain.

"Whew!" Ranger said with a snort. "This is one big bad storm. Let's stay here until it passes."

"I agree," the palomino said with a nod of his head.

The storm passed quickly. As the sun peeked from beneath the layer of clouds, a rainbow appeared in the sky. The huge arch was vivid in color from pale yellow to pink to red to lavender to dark purple.

"Wow, look!" the dappled grey murmured. "That is beautiful."

"Yes, it is," Ranger said quietly. "And I believe it means good luck."

The other horses snickered as Ranger slowly walked from beneath the shed.

"That's silly," the roan scoffed. "It doesn't mean good luck. It's just something that happens after a rain."

"A rainbow doesn't show up after every storm," the sorrel said. "Sometimes it appears, and sometimes it doesn't. There is some kind of scientific reason for it happening, but I don't know what it is."

"Well, now," the roan snorted. "Whether it shows up or not doesn't mean good luck."

"We'll see," the sorrel said in a quiet voice. "Ranger believes it will bring good luck, and I think he's a pretty smart horse."

Murmurs of agreement echoed from beneath the shed as the horses slowly walked into the large corral where Ranger was standing.

By late afternoon the sun was shining brightly. "Hmmm," Ranger thought as he looked into the clear blue sky. "This has turned into one beautiful day. I just wonder what lucky thing is going to happen?" Then he heard the ranch foreman walking toward the corral. He was talking in a serious tone of voice to another man.

"Welcome, stranger," Ranger nickered loudly. "Isn't it a beautiful afternoon?"

The ranch foreman laughed and then pointed to Ranger. "That's the olive grullo I was telling you about, Mr. Pinkerton."

"Call me Allan," the man said.

"Allan Pinkerton," Ranger said. "Maybe he is my good luck from the rainbow."

Allan Pinkerton made a quick check of the olive grullo, then gave a nod of his head.

The ranch foreman looked at Allan in silence for a moment before clearing his throat and asking, "Did you say that you are from Chicago?"

Allan Pinkerton nodded his head and replied, "Yes, I am."

"And," the foreman continued, "you'll be going back there when you find the right horse to buy?"

Again, Allan nodded.

The foreman said, "I have two horses to pick up in Chicago to bring back for training. Would you mind if I traveled with you?"

"That would be my pleasure," Allan replied with a smile. "The miles seem to go by pretty slow when a fellow travels by himself."

"Oh!" Ranger thought. "This is my lucky day. Now I can leave here with an old friend and a new boss!"

Less than three hours later, Ranger the olive grullo was on his way to Chicago, Illinois, with his new boss, Allan Pinkerton, the Rocking S Ranch foreman, and the dappled grey. While trotting up the lane to leave, he glanced at his friends in the corral. All but the roan nickered a farewell.

"Humph," the roan grumbled. "I still don't believe there is good luck in a rainbow."

"Well," Ranger nickered, "if you don't believe that good luck will be coming to you, it won't happen. Well, good-bye, my friends." Then he added, "Good luck to all of you!"

## Two

# Horse Thief Caught!

Late the next day, the sun was setting on the western horizon as Ranger, Allan Pinkerton, the ranch foreman, and the dappled grey stopped for the night. The two men immediately started a campfire and began preparing some food.

"Now, this has been a fun trip," Ranger said as he took a bite of oats.

"Yes, I guess it has," the grey replied. "But we are only on the second day. I heard my boss say that Chicago is a week away."

"Good!" the olive grullo said with a nicker. "I'm excited about seeing new country and meeting new friends."

"It's just a lot of walking and trotting to me," the grey mumbled.

Ranger glared at him a second, then snorted, "You'll have fun if you allow it. I'm having a lot of fun just listening to the ranch foreman and Boss visit. Did you hear him telling the ranch foreman about how he and his wife were shipwrecked on their way from Glasgow, Scotland?"

"Yes, I did," the grey said with a nod of his head. "That was a wild way to introduce his new bride to America, wasn't it?"

Ranger chuckled and pawed the ground with one front hoof.

"See, Grey?" he muttered.

"Boss had good luck because his new bride did not go right back to Scotland without him!"

"Ranger," the grey said quietly, "he calls himself a cooper. What is a cooper?"

The olive grullo chuckled and said, "Don't feel bad because you didn't know what a cooper does. I didn't know either until he described making wooden barrels with his dad. That's one thing he does. He owns a cooperage."

"Folks use wooden barrels for water, don't they?" the grey asked.

"Yes," Ranger replied with a nod of his head. "They use them for water and vinegar and pickles and a whole bunch of other things."

"Hmmm," the grey murmured. "Sounds like an important business."

"It is," the olive grullo agreed. "But his detective business sounds more interesting to me. Now, that's going to be fun and very exciting." Ranger yawned real big and then murmured, "Well, good night, Grey. We better get some sleep. We have a lot of miles to travel tomorrow."

Smack-dab in the middle of the night, the olive grullo was suddenly awakened by a strange sound. Then he felt his halter rope being untied.

"Come on, you ornery horse," a voice whispered. "Let's get out of here before those fellows wake up."

The olive grullo jerked his head up, but the man held firmly to the halter rope.

"I told you to come with me," he said in a gruff voice.

"No!" Ranger nickered. "You are not my boss. My boss is asleep, and I'm not going anywhere with you."

The man pulled a short whip from his hind pocket and shook it.

"You are coming with me," he whispered through clenched teeth, "or I am going to use this on you."

"Oh, no you won't!" Ranger nickered as he pawed the air with his front hooves.

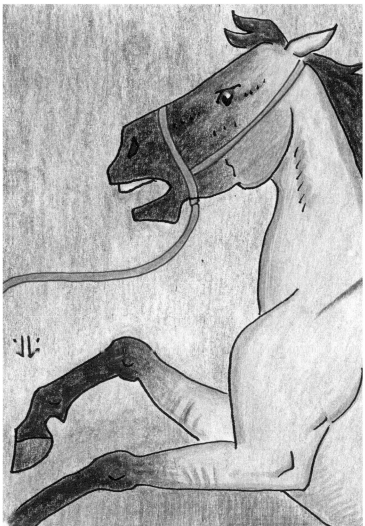

Allan Pinkerton's slow deep voice said, "Stop where you are. Put the whip down, and turn my horse loose."

"I wasn't going to steal him," the man said meekly. "I just wanted a better look at him. That's all."

"Huh?" Ranger gasped. "You sure do have a funny way of getting acquainted, mister."

"If you let me go," the horse thief said, "I'll tell you about a ring of counterfeiters. They're a lot more dangerous than I am."

Allan Pinkerton nodded his head and said, "Keep talking. If you are telling the truth, I may work with you."

"Oh, Boss," Ranger murmured. "This guy is a horse thief. He's a very bad man! Don't make deals with him."

## Three

# Plot to Assassinate Lincoln

Later, Ranger understood the reason that his boss wanted to catch the counterfeiters more than a horse thief.

A tear of pride trickled down Ranger's face as he watched the City of Chicago appoint Allan Pinkerton as its very first detective. "Hmmm," he thought. "First you were a cooper. Then you were a Cook County deputy sheriff. Now you are Chicago's first detective. Wow! I'm real proud of you, Boss."

As they were on their way home one evening, Allan suddenly said, "Ranger, this is 1851, a time for progress. I'm going to start a detective agency. I'll call it the Pinkerton Detective Agency, and it will be the best detective firm in the nation."

The olive grullo nodded his head and whinnied, "I believe you, Boss. And I also believe that you will have the best detective agency in the whole wide world!"

"Train robbers," Allan said, "are a real problem right now. Those outlaws are robbing the folks and stealing the mail. I'm going to try to get a contract to protect the railways."

"That's a great idea, Boss," Ranger neighed excitedly. "That big rainbow is still giving me good luck in exciting adventures." Lifting his head high, he pranced proudly up the street toward home. He murmured, "Wish my old Rocking S friends could see me now."

For the next several years, Ranger, Allan, and all the hired Pinkerton detectives traveled the roadways and railways catching bad guys. The Pinkerton Detective Agency quickly became famous throughout the country.

One night, Ranger was sound asleep in his stall when he suddenly heard the barn door open. He looked around and saw his boss walking toward him.

"Wow, Boss," the olive grullo nickered softly, "you sure look tired. Why aren't you in bed?"

Allan groaned quietly as he sat down on a bale of hay.

"I have learned about a plot," he said to Ranger, "to assassinate president-elect Abraham Lincoln when he arrives in Baltimore."

"You can stop him from going to Baltimore," Ranger suggested.

"But," Allan continued, "some folks don't believe me. They think I'm making up this story to gain glory for my detective agency."

"I think you should protect president-elect Lincoln," Ranger whinnied quietly. "What if the plot is true, and he gets murdered because you didn't warn him?"

Allan suddenly stood up and squared his shoulders.

"I'm going to have him change his schedule," he said in a firm voice. "That's the safe thing to do!"

The olive grullo nickered, "You have caught hundreds of thieves, train robbers, and outlaws over the past years. You are the very best detective in the whole wide world."

Ranger felt good as the man stroked his neck before leaving the barn. He watched Allan hesitate at the door. Then turning around to face the olive grullo, he smiled.

"You, Ranger," he said quietly, "are the best partner a detective could ever want. It was one lucky day for me when I found you on the Rocking S Horse Ranch. Well, good night, my friend and colleague."

As the door closed behind him, Ranger shivered with happiness. "Hmmm," he thought. "I must be the luckiest horse in the world. My boss is Allan Pinkerton, owner of the famous Pinkerton Detective Agency, and my life is filled with catching bad guys and protecting good folks. My boss will go down in history as a great investigator."

Ranger sighed, "I wonder if folks will remember Allan Pinkerton's olive grullo named Ranger. Oh well, I guess it doesn't really matter if they do or not. My life is wonderful and exciting anyway!"

# Four

## Olive Grullo Facts

*Grullo* is a Spanish name for the sandhill crane, a slate-colored bird. The term is used by cowboys when they are referring to a blue, slate-colored horse with black points and a dark or black head.

Grullo horses have primitive marks (dorsal stripe, withers stripe, and stripes over the hocks and knees).

When the slate-colored body hairs are mixed with black, the horse will have black points and a dark head, with a body color more yellow than that of most other grullos. It is called an olive grullo because the color is close to an unripe olive.

## Olive Grullo

# BEYOND "THE END"

*I love the horse from hoof to head.*
*From head to hoof and tail to mane.*
*I love the horse as I have said –*
*From head to hoof and back again.*
James Whitcomb Riley

## WORD LIST

| | |
|---|---|
| grullo | hoof |
| grey | halter |
| sorrel | hay |
| clippers | roan |
| whip | stripe |
| palomino | Morgan |
| neck | oats |
| body brush | |

From the word list on page 37, write:

1. One word that names a breed of horse.

2. One word that tells a mark on a horse.

3. Two words that are points of a horse.

4. Two words that are tack articles.

5. Two words that are grooming articles.

6. Two words that are food for a horse.

7. Five words that tell the color of a horse. Put these five words in alphabetical order.

# CURRICULUM CONNECTIONS

Was Allan Pinkerton a real person? Is this a true story? Is it based on true facts—something that really happened? (Yes, so it is a historical fiction story.) Where was Allan Pinkerton born? Where did he live when he came to America? Why was he called a cooper? What important branch of the U.S. Army did he organize during the Civil War? Find these answers and more about him at web site <www.wtv-zone.com/civilwar/apinkerton.html>.

Where is the sun when you see a rainbow?

Find Baltimore on a map. What state is Baltimore in? How far is Baltimore from Springfield, Illinois? How are Baltimore, Springfield, and Abraham Lincoln connected?

## PROJECT

Combine your math and artistic skills! Draw to scale and accurately color a picture (body, tail, and mane) of the horse that is featured in each book read in the Saddle Up Series. You could soon have sixty horses prancing around the walls of your classroom!

**Learning + horses = FUN**.

Look in your school library media center for books about how to draw a horse and the colors of horses. Don't forget the useful information in the last chapter of this book (Olive Grullo Facts) and the picture on the book cover for a shape and color guide.

HELPFUL HINTS AND WEBSITES

A horse is measured in hands. One hand equals four inches. Use a scale of 1" equals 1 hand.

Visit website <www.equisearch.com> to find a glossary of equine terms, information about tack and equipment, breeds, art and graphics, and more about horses. Learn more at <www.horse-country. com> and at <www.ansi.okstate.edu/breeds/horses/>.

KidsClick! is a web search for kids by librarians. There are many interesting websites here. HORSES and HORSE-MANSHIP are two of the more than 600 subjects. Visit <www.kidsclick.org>.

Is your classroom beginning to look like the Rocking S Horse Ranch? Happy Trails to You!

ANSWERS (1. Yes. 2. Allan Pinkerton was born in Scotland, settled near Chicago and was a barrel maker or cooper. He organized the Secret Service for the U.S. Army. 3. The sun will be behind you.  4. Baltimore is in Maryland.  5. The cities are 787 road miles apart, according to website <www. freetrip. com>.  6. Lincoln left Springfield in 1861 for his inauguration in Washington and traveled through Baltimore, where Pinkerton foiled a plot to murder him.)